FAVORITE DOG BREEDS

LABRADOR RETRIEVERS

by Martha E. H. Rustad

AMICUS HIGH INTEREST • AMICUS INK

Amicus High Interest and Amicus Ink are imprints of Amicus
P.O. Box 227, Mankato, MN 56002
www.amicuspublishing.us

Library of Congress Cataloging-in-Publication Data
Names: Rustad, Martha E. H. (Martha Elizabeth Hillman), 1975- author.
Title: Labrador retrievers / by Martha E. H. Rustad.
Description: Mankato, Minnesota : Amicus High Interest/Amicus Ink, [2018] | Series: Favorite dog breeds | Audience: K to grade 3. | Includes bibliographical references and index.
Identifiers: LCCN 2016034044 (print) | LCCN 2016045102 (ebook) | ISBN 9781681511283 (library binding) | ISBN 9781681521596 (pbk.) | ISBN 9781681512181 (ebook)
Subjects: LCSH: Labrador retriever--Juvenile literature. | Hunting dogs--Juvenile literature. | Working dogs--Juvenile literature. | Dog breeds--Juvenile literature.
Classification: LCC SF429.L3 R87 2018 (print) | LCC SF429.L3 (ebook) | DDC 636.752/7--dc23
LC record available at https://lccn.loc.gov/2016034044

Photo Credits: paolo airenti/Shutterstock cover; Susan Schmitz/Shutterstock 2, 8-9; stuart.renneberg/Shutterstock 4-5; Mary Evans Picture Library 6-7; flyfloor/iStock/PW 6-7; Annette Shaff/Shutterstock 10-11; Darwin Wiggett/Collection: First Light/AgeFotostock 12-13; otsphoto/Shutterstock 14; Viorel Sima/Shutterstock 16-17; Cylonphoto/iStock 18; Roberto A Sanchez/iStock 20-21; Eric Isselee/Shutterstock 22

Editor: Wendy Dieker
Designer: Tracy Myers
Photo Researcher: Holly Young

TABLE OF CONTENTS

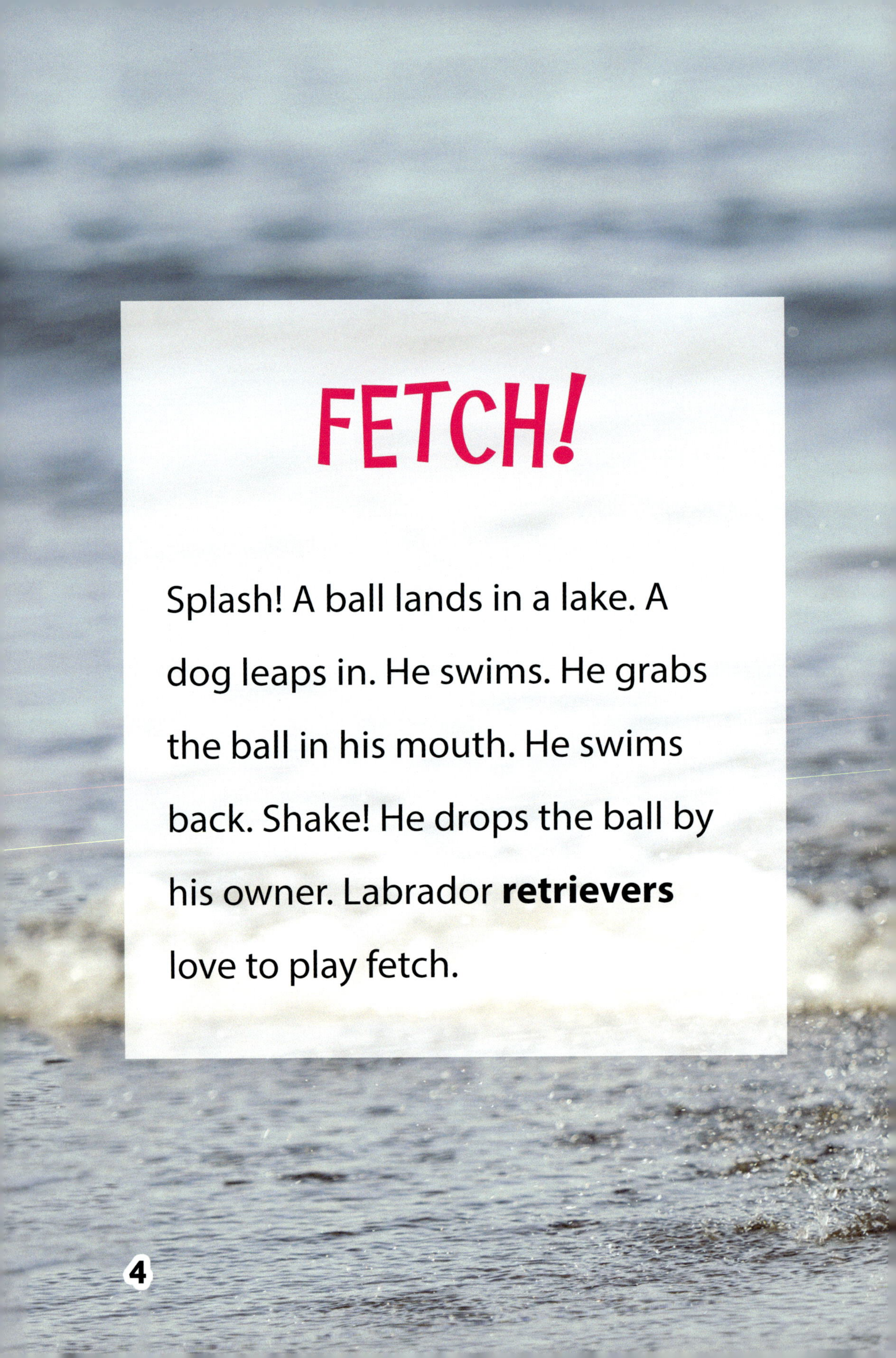

FETCH!

Splash! A ball lands in a lake. A dog leaps in. He swims. He grabs the ball in his mouth. He swims back. Shake! He drops the ball by his owner. Labrador **retrievers** love to play fetch.

FISHER DOGS

The Labrador retriever **breed** came from Canada. These dogs jumped out of boats. They swam to get fisher's nets. Today, the Lab is the most popular dog breed in the United States.

WATERPROOF COAT

Labs have short, thick fur. Oil keeps their coat from getting too wet. They dry quickly. This coat also helps them keep warm in the rain. They shake off the water.

Furry Fact

Labs come in three colors. They are black, chocolate, and yellow. Yellow labs could be any color from nearly white to red.

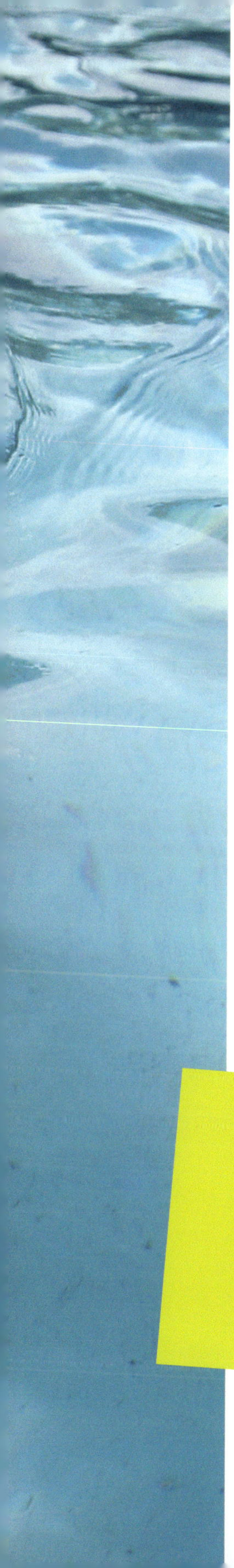

SWIMMING DOGS

Labs are built to swim. They have **webbed** toes. Their feet act like paddles. Labs have thick, strong tails. The tail works like a **rudder**. It helps steer in water.

Furry Fact

Puppies don't know how to swim when they are born. They have to learn, just like people do.

STRONG NOSE, GENTLE MOUTH

Labrador retrievers have a strong sense of smell. They sniff and find things for their owners. Labs carry things in their mouths. They do not bite down hard. They do not hurt the things they carry.

Furry Fact

A Lab can carry an egg in its gentle mouth without breaking it.

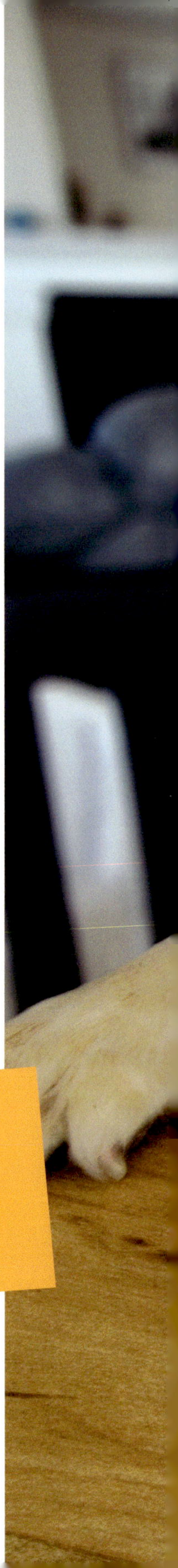

POWERFUL MUSCLES

Labs have **muscular** bodies. Labs run fast on their strong legs. Jump! Their powerful back legs push their large bodies off the ground.

Furry Fact

Labs can jump far. Some dogs run and jump off docks into lakes.

PUPPIES

A Lab **litter** has about eight puppies. The pups can each be a different color. A pup can be a different color than its mom or dad. Owners don't always know what color the puppies will be.

TRAINED FOR WORK

Labrador retrievers are smart dogs. They can be trained for many jobs. Labs work as **guide dogs** for people who are blind. They also learn how to find missing people.

Furry Fact

Some Labs work with police. Their strong noses can sniff for drugs.

FAMILY FRIEND

Labs are kind dogs. They are friendly. They welcome everyone. These dogs play gently with kids. They seem to smile at their families. Labrador retrievers are good pets.

Furry Fact

Labs do not make good guard dogs. They seem to like everyone.

HOW DO YOU KNOW IT'S A LABRADOR RETRIEVER?

WORDS TO KNOW

breed – a dog that has certain features that make it different from other kinds of dogs

guide dog – a dog trained to lead a person who can't see well

litter – a group of puppies born at the same time

muscular – to have lots of muscles and strength

retriever – a dog that fetches things and brings them back to its owner

rudder – a flat plate on the back of a boat that is used to steer in water

webbed – having extra skin between the toes

LEARN MORE

Books

Barnes, Nico. *Labrador Retrievers.* Dogs. Minneapolis: Abdo Kids, 2015.

Bowman, Chris. *Labrador Retrievers.* Awesome Dogs. Minneapolis: Bellwether Media, 2016.

Websites

American Kennel Club: Labrador Retriever
http://www.akc.org/dog-breeds/labrador-retriever/

Dog Breed Info Center: Labrador Retriever Pictures
http://www.dogbreedinfo.com/labradorphotos.htm

INDEX